In memory of

Clara Brogini

Giuliano's wife and founder of Casa dei Bambini,
a Montessori school in Rome where
she pioneered teaching the very young

www.enchantedlion.com

First Edition published in 2021 by Enchanted Lion Books
248 Creamer Street, Studio 4, Brooklyn, New York 11231
Text copyright © 2021 by John Miller
Illustrations copyright © 2021 by the family of Giuliano Cucco
Art Direction: Claudia Zoe Bedrick
All rights reserved under International and Pan-American Copyright Conventions
A CIP record is on file with the Library of Congress
ISBN: 978-1-59270-361-6

Printed in Italy by Società Editoriale Grafiche AZ
First Printing

Before I Grew Up

John Miller · Giuliano Cucco

Enchanted Lion Books
NEW YORK

My name is Giuliano Cucco, and this is a portrait of me as a grown-up.
But this story is about me as a child, before I grew up and became an artist.

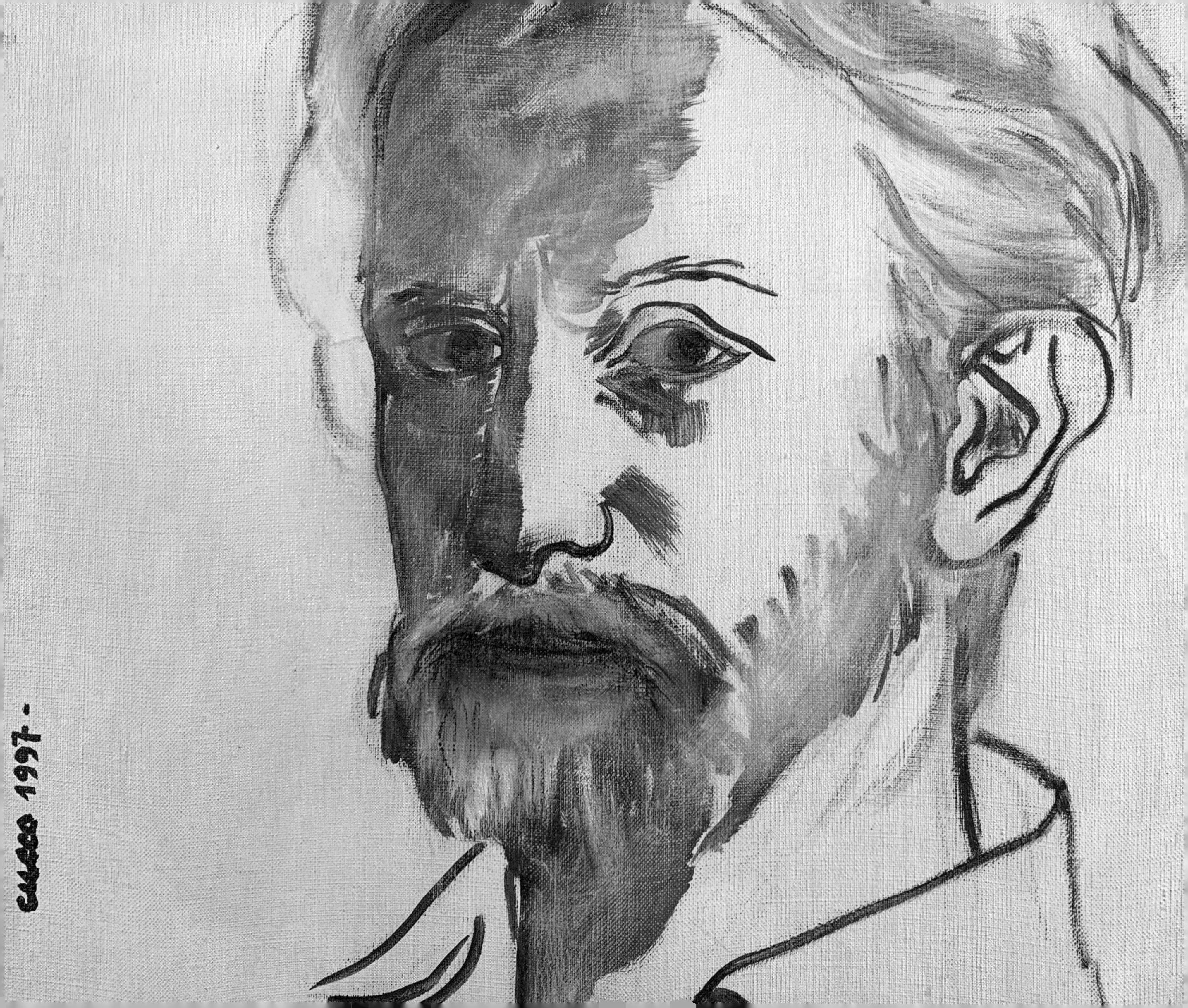

My mother was tall and very beautiful. She talked to me a lot, especially when she stood before her oval mirror.

We invented a game with a yellow rag doll. I would hold up the frame of her mirror, and she would try to toss the doll through it. I would keep score.

We played this game over and over, until my uncle, aunt, and the family priest, who came to dinner every Sunday, grew tired of watching and said they had to go.

In my room, I had my own workbench, where I made paper boats and let them float away like dreams.

In some of my dreams, I'd scooter after my boats, up into the sky.

Other dreams were dark and scary.

My father was a scientist who studied where light came from—
not sunlight, but another kind of light he said was inaccessible.

He didn't talk much.
He preferred to ride his bicycle to the ocean ...

...and row out among the waves
in a tippy row boat, looking for the light.

I preferred to go to my mother's garden, to watch the tulips open.

There, I was never lonely.

Sometimes, I would dream that I could float into the sky like a bird, up and away from my mother's garden.

But my mother also wanted to acquaint me with city life, so she sent me to stay with my aunt and uncle.

I found a hobbyhorse in their attic and charged through the living room, scaring everyone.

In the same attic, I found a wooden box.
When I opened it, a moon shot out and rose into the sky.

In the city, I saw a red-robed priest on a swing...

...and a champion bowler, who could knock down all ten pins with one roll.

I also saw some people on the street tugging at cords.
They said they were trying to keep their balloon from blowing away,
but to me, it looked like a person.

In the city, I once released a dove from my aunt's balcony.
I didn't want it to be served for dinner like the rest.

Life in the city was strange and exciting, but I was glad to return to the country.

Once again, I could wander along the path between the two neighboring houses...

...and climb to the top of the tower of the third.

I could go fly my kite.

One evening, when I was about twelve years old, my father carried his oars down to the water and rowed out looking for the light he said was inaccessible.

When he returned home,
he said the ocean was so calm
that he stood up and played his violin.

Here's a picture I painted from what he told me.
After, I asked him if I had painted the light he was seeking.

My father wasn't much of a talker, but this time he
said these three words: "Yes, you did."

That was enough.

From then on, I knew I would grow up to be an artist.

How this book came about

Of course, Giuliano Cucco did not paint these pictures when he was a young boy. Instead, it took him years and years of adulthood to be able to paint so well. I discovered these paintings, along with many others, when I went back to Rome, where I had lived as a young man fifty years ago. At that time, Giuliano and I had worked closely on four children's books, which were never published because reproducing full-color illustrations was too expensive back then. But fifty years later, things had changed, and Enchanted Lion was eager to publish our books. I couldn't wait to bring the good news to my long-lost friend!

After a long hunt for Giuliano, I heard from his sister-in-law that in 2006, Giuliano and his wife had died in a traffic accident in Rome. I then made contact with their son, Giovanni, who was cataloging the large trove of his father's paintings, most of which had never been exhibited and many of which depicted his father's early boyhood. From the latter, I assembled this story of his childhood, trying to keep as close as possible to Giuliano's voice and spirit. Most often picture books start with a story and the pictures follow, but here the pictures took the lead in revealing and telling Giuliano's story.

– John Miller